If I Could Drive a

BULLDOZER!

by Michael Teitelbaum
Illustrated by Uldis Klavins

SCHOLASTIC INC.

New York   Toronto   London   Auckland   Sydney
Mexico City   New Delhi   Hong Kong   Buenos Aires

TONKA™ is a trademark of Hasbro, Inc.
Used with permission.
Copyright © 2002 Hasbro, Inc.
All rights reserved. Published by Scholastic Inc.
SCHOLASTIC and associated logos are trademarks and/or registered trademarks of Scholastic Inc.

Library of Congress Cataloging-in-Publication Data

Teitelbaum, Michael.
    If I could drive a bulldozer! / by Michael Teitelbaum; illustrated by Uldis Klavins
        p. cm.
Summary: A young boy describes all the work he would do if he drove a bulldozer.
ISBN 0-439-34175-2 (pbk.)
    [1. Bulldozers -- Fiction.] I. title: Tonka, if I could drive a bulldozer. II. Klavins, Uldis, ill. III. Title.

PZ7.T233 Ie 2002
[E]--dc21   2001042039

ISBN 0-439-34175-2

10 9 8 7 6 5 4 3 2 1   02 03 04 05 06

Printed in the U.S.A.
First Scholastic printing, May 2002

My name is Matt, and I
really love playing with trucks.

My favorite truck is the
bulldozer.

I play with my toy bulldozer
in the backyard, pushing dirt
and rocks around.

Sometimes I pretend that my bulldozer is knocking down an old building to make room for a new one.

What if *I* could drive a bulldozer?

A bulldozer can weigh as much as ten tons! It is like a tank with a large steel blade on the front.

A bulldozer doesn't have wheels. It rolls on special crawler treads.

The treads make it easy for the bulldozer to roll over rough ground. They also help hold up the bulldozer's heavy weight. That way, the weight is spread over a big area, so the bulldozer doesn't sink into the mud.

My bulldozer's sharp blade stays close to the ground, cutting through even the hardest soil.

The blade can be raised, lowered, or even tilted to reach just the right angle.

Because of its crawler treads, a bulldozer can't ride on the road like other trucks. I drive my bulldozer onto the back of a big truck called a tractor trailer. Then the tractor trailer drives along paved roads, carrying the bulldozer.

That's how I get my bulldozer to the job site.

At the job site, I drive my bulldozer down the tractor trailer's ramp. Now it's ready to work.

Usually, my bulldozer is the first truck at the site. It prepares the site so that other trucks can do their jobs.

Today I am helping a farmer by knocking down his old barn. Then I'll help prepare the site for a new barn to be built.

The old barn was starting to fall down on its own, and it was too dangerous to use anymore. Working carefully, my bulldozer helps to push down the rest of the crumbling building.

Then I push the broken pieces of the barn away to make room for the new one.

Finally, I use the bottom of the bulldozer's blade to push the dirt and smooth out the ground.
    Now the new barn can be built!

The bulldozer's work is done now.
    Some other trucks arrive. Here comes a
loader to scoop, a backhoe to dig, and a dump
truck to carry away the wood from the old barn.